BEASTS
—OF—
OLYMPUS

For Faith, who reads enough books
to feed a griffin

GROSSET & DUNLAP
Published by the Penguin Group
Penguin Group (USA) LLC, 375 Hudson Street, New York, New York 10014, USA

USA | Canada | UK | Ireland | Australia | New Zealand | India | South Africa | China

penguin.com
A Penguin Random House Company

The publisher does not have any control over and does not assume any responsibility
for author or third-party websites or their content.

Text copyright © 2015 by Lucy Coats. Illustrations copyright © 2015 by Brett Bean. All rights reserved.
Published by Grosset & Dunlap, a division of Penguin Young Readers Group, 345 Hudson Street, New York,
New York 10014. GROSSET & DUNLAP is a trademark of Penguin Group (USA) LLC. Printed in the USA.

Library of Congress Cataloging-in-Publication Data is available.

ISBN 978-0-448-46195-3   10 9 8 7 6 5 4 3 2 1

BEASTS

—OF— OLYMPUS

by Lucy Coats   art by Brett Bean

Steeds of the Gods

GROSSET & DUNLAP
An Imprint of Penguin Group (USA) LLC

CHAPTER 1

THE GOD FROM THE SEA

Demon first found out about his latest Important
Visitor when he heard Melanie the naiad shriek.
He dropped his shovel in the poo barrow and
rushed over to the spring outside the Stables of the
Gods to see what was happening. Melanie stood
shivering and curtsying at the side of her spring,
her long blue hair streaming down her back. In the
middle of the water stood a huge bearded figure
wearing a crown of jeweled seashells. He held a
large golden trident in his left hand.

"Pah!" he spat, wringing out his robes and striding up to Demon. "Freshwater. Mimsy-flimsy stuff. Give me a pool of salty sea brine any day."

Demon's heart sank into his sandals as he bowed

low. An early morning visit from a god was never good news—and this was Zeus's own brother. What could Poseidon, god of the sea, want with him at this hour?

"How can I help you, Your Watery Wondrousness?" he asked.

"Ha!" said Poseidon, bringing his hand down on Demon's shoulder so hard, the young boy fell on his backside in the dust. "Watery Wondrousness. I like it. Up you get, now, stable boy. I need to talk to you." He reached down and offered a hand wearing a glove that seemed to be made of sapphires the size and shape of barnacles. Demon took the hand cautiously. It felt cold and rather wet, and the jewel barnacles scraped his fingers, but he didn't say anything. It was best not to with gods. They took offense very easily, he'd found, and that could lead to Bad Things.

Poseidon was looking around him. The nine

green heads of Doris the Hydra were peering shyly around the Stables' door, long eyelashes fluttering. Demon could see the griffin lurking behind them.

"That the beastie you cured for Hera?" the god asked. "Looks pretty healthy to me."

"Yes, Your Serene Saltiness," said Demon. "It helps me out around the Stables now." Doris fluttered its eighteen sets of eyelashes and rattled its buckets.

"Snackies?" Doris asked hopefully. Demon ignored it. He'd only just cured its bellyache from eating too much ambrosia cake, and he wasn't risking a repeat.

"Show me around, stable boy," said Poseidon.

Demon took the god up and down the stalls. He warned him politely not to poke at the giant scorpion with the pointy end of his trident, and explained about the Cattle of the Sun not being able to eat ambrosia cake because of the terrible gas it gave them. By the time they'd almost finished, Demon was feeling a bit more optimistic. Poseidon seemed much friendlier than the scary Hera, and a lot nicer than sinister Hades. Demon shivered, remembering his recent trip down to the Underworld to save the life of Hades's great beastdog, Cerberus. He'd only just escaped being eaten by the King of Death's skeleton dragons, thanks to the help of Hermes, the gods' chief messenger. Stopping at the last pen, he gestured at the creatures within.

"These are the Ethiopian winged horses, Your Royal Godnificence," he said, patting the shiny golden horns in the middle of the boss horse's forehead. "I fly out on Keith here most days—they need a lot of exercise to keep their wings strong." Keith neighed enthusiastically.

"What do you know of Hippocamps, stable boy?" Poseidon asked abruptly. Demon racked his brain. Hippocamps? What in the name of Zeus's toenails were they?

"I-I-I've never met one, Your Outstanding Oceanosity," he said.

"No. I suppose you wouldn't have. I don't bring them up here much—no proper seawater, you see." He clapped his hands together. "You'll just have to come back to the Stables of the Ocean with me and examine them. Their scales are all falling off, and none of my sea people seem to know why." Demon gulped and turned pale. He didn't know what to do. How could he leave his own Stables again? If there was no one to clean them out and look after the beasts, the whole of Olympus would smell of poo. Then the goddesses would get furious and turn him into one big Demon-size pile of ash. Poseidon frowned, his shaggy eyebrows throwing off silvery-green sparks.

"You don't seem very happy, stable boy," he

growled. The atmosphere in the Stables had suddenly become heavy and close, as if a big thunderstorm was coming. The winged horses whinnied in alarm as gusts of wind began to whip the dust up into mini-tornadoes. Demon hurriedly forced a smile onto his face. He should have known that Poseidon's nice mood was too good to last.

"N-no, n-no, Your Awesome Aquaticness. I-I-I was just w-wondering what medicines to bring. I-I'll go and fetch my box immediately."

"Very well," said Poseidon, his frown disappearing as suddenly as it had come. "I'll go and visit with my brother Zeus. I have a small matter I need to discuss with him. Be ready when I return." With a swish and a swirl of his still-dripping cloak, he left the Stables, depositing a small pile of flapping fish and a large, angry lobster at Demon's feet. The boy leaped out of reach of the lobster's clacking claws and ran for the hospital shed. The griffin, after it had gobbled up the fish, loped after him on its lion's feet.

"Dearie me, Pan's scrawny kid," it sniggered, when it had caught up with him. "Looks like you're in trouble, whichever way you jump."

"I know," Demon panted as he ran. "What am I going to DO, Griffin? I can't just leave all of you on your own again. Look what happened with Doris last time. And what do I do if he keeps me down there for ages? Aphrodite will probably turn me into a pile of burnt rose petals if her nighties start to smell of poo again."

"We-e-e-ll," said the griffin slowly, "I suppose the Nemean Lion and I could make sure Doris cleans out the stables and doesn't eat all the ambrosia cake again. Lion's been a bit depressed since you gave it that fluffy green skin. It'll cheer it up no end to have a job to do."

"Would you really?" asked Demon as he skidded

to a halt in front of the hospital shed. "I don't think it'll take very long. I'll be back in a day or so, I swear." The griffin looked at him slyly out of the corner of its orange eye.

"If you'll promise to give me meat at least once a week when you get back," it said. "Otherwise the deal's off." Demon groaned. Meat was really hard to come by on Olympus, unless it was a feast day. But he didn't really have a choice. He'd think about how to get around the griffin's request when he got back. If Poseidon hadn't turned him into a Demon-shaped coral reef by then, of course.

"All RIGHT!" he said crossly. "But you have to do the job properly. I don't want to find a piece of hay out of place or a single speck of dust in any of the stalls. And I especially don't want to find Doris sick again. Understand?"

"Trust me, Pan's scrawny kid," it said, giving Demon a sideways orange wink that made it look most UNtrustworthy. Then it flapped its eagle wings once and soared up to sit on the rooftop. "Better hurry up," it called down. "I see old Fishface coming out of Zeus's palace. He doesn't look in a very good mood."

Demon's magical medicine box didn't turn out to be in a very good mood, either, when he told it they were going to Poseidon's realm. He could hear it grumbling behind him as it waddled its way toward the Stables on its short, stumpy legs.

"Shut up, box," Demon hissed as he saw Poseidon in the distance. "You'll get us into trouble."

"Implementing aquasynchrous marine interface," it muttered. "As for you, I hope you get Error Code 7533 and turn into a sea cucumber." It withdrew its legs and thumped down beside him, ejecting a kind of see-through skin from its sides, which spread over its whole surface, sealing it completely. Demon stared at it. How was he supposed to open it now? But he had no time to think about that, because Poseidon was stomping toward him, muttering to himself. The air became thick and still again, and there was a strong smell of ozone.

"Come with me, stable boy," the god said, gripping Demon's arm with his barnacle-gloved hand and, without another word, pulling him toward Melanie's spring. Demon grabbed onto the box's now-slightly-sticky-feeling handle and tugged. Slipping and sliding, it bounced behind him as he was dragged into the pool, sinking rapidly downward before he could take more than one panicked, gasping breath of air.

CHAPTER 2
THE STABLES OF THE OCEAN

Demon held his breath for as long as he could, but eventually long streamers of silvery bubbles began to gush out of his mouth. He kicked and struggled against the god's hold as he took in a big breath of seawater. Choking, his vision began to go black at the edges. *I'm going to drown*, he thought. Just then, Poseidon turned to look at him, godly green eyes flashing as they took in what was happening. Whirling his trident around in one swift movement, he pointed it at Demon. Bright purple streaks shot

out of its three golden tips and weaved themselves
swiftly into a net that dropped over Demon's head
and body. It encased him completely before it sank
into his skin and disappeared.

"Yurrch! Yech! Yuck!" he wheezed, hacking up
seawater and snot from the bottom of his lungs.
Offy and Yukus, the two snakes that made up his
magical healing necklace, curled and uncurled
themselves anxiously around his neck. Demon just
hoped they weren't going to get any ideas about
plunging down his throat to suck the rest of the
water out.

"You weedy earthbound half-mortals," said

Poseidon as they started to zoom downward through the dark water again. "No stamina, that's your trouble. You'll be all right now that I've given you some of my sea power."

Just as Demon was getting used to the strange sensation of breathing water as if it were air, his heart gave a panicky thump. With all the coughing and drowning, he'd somehow let go of his magic healing box. He craned desperately over one shoulder. A flash of silver caught his eye, just as he felt a bump at the back of his knees. The box had developed silvery fins and was swimming clumsily at his heels. He closed his eyes in relief.

Annoying as it was, there was no way he was going to cure a Hippocamp without its help. Whatever a Hippocamp was.

"Follow me, stable boy," said Poseidon as they landed on the ocean floor. He swam off toward a rocky mountain covered in silver seaweed, with Demon dog-paddling awkwardly behind him. He wasn't used to swimming so fast, and rather wished he could grow fins like the box had. Quite soon he saw a wash of blue-green light in front of him. Two enormous golden doors stood open at the entrance to the mountain. They were guarded by two brawny creatures, half man, half fish, who thumped their spears on the ground and snapped to rigid, tail-quivering attention as Poseidon stalked past. Demon and the box hurried along at his side.

"All hail the Father of Oceans! All hail the King of the Seas," they shouted out in a dreary monotone, making Demon jump.

"Yes, yes," said Poseidon testily. "No need for all that." He bent his head down toward Demon. "My guards, the Tritons, have loyal hearts but few brains. Now, come on, stable boy. My poor Hippocamps won't get any better if you just stand there gaping." Demon began to hear a rustling, scraping sort of sound, and as they turned a rocky corner, he saw a series of nine stalls made from what looked like multicolored coral. Every stall was filled with a very odd-looking beast. Each had a shiny, smooth-skinned white horse head and chest, and front legs that ended in dinner plate–size hooves surrounded by a ruff of spiny fins. Their backs and hindquarters were like monstrous fish, and their long, golden, spike-finned manes waved in the watery current. Demon could see the problem immediately. The round greenish-bronze scales that covered their rear ends were ragged and torn. Each Hippocamp had big, pink, raw-looking patches where there were no scales at all.

"Oh! You poor things," said Demon, walking over to pat the nearest one, which promptly reared, squealed with rage, and bared its large square teeth at him. "Stop that," he said in his firmest beast-taming voice. "I'm here to help you."

"Make them comfortable, stable boy," ordered Poseidon. "Find out what's wrong and fix it. You may ask one of the Tritons to bring you up to the throne room when you're finished. I have a meeting with Helios to go to now." He paused, frowning, as a cloud of tiny golden fish zipped in and out of his beard. "Can't think what my wretched sky cousin wants with me. Fire and water don't mix, you know." With that, he launched himself upward and shot through a hole in the ceiling. Demon sighed. Although the sea god hadn't threatened to turn him into a pile of burnt seaweed, nobody needed to tell him that things wouldn't go well for him if he didn't find a cure for the Hippocamps.

"Right, box," he said, turning around. "We have work to do. Let's find out what's wrong with these poor beasts." But the box had disappeared. "Box!" he said again, peering into the dark corners of the Stables of the Ocean. "Box! Stop sulking and come here at once." There was no reply. Trying not to panic, Demon looked into every stall and checked behind every rock. Then he swam back down the passage to the golden doors. "Have you seen my silver box?" he asked the Tritons. They shook their heads. Demon wanted to kick something. He wished he'd never taken on this stupid job. He was swimming back toward the Stables of the Ocean, thinking gloomy thoughts about all the horrible things Poseidon was going to do to him now, when he heard a shout behind him.

"Lost something?" asked a high little voice. Paddling around clumsily, he saw a girl in a blue floaty robe. She had two braids of long dark-green hair wound around her head, firmly clipped in place by several pairs of golden crabs; very pale green skin; and legs that ended in two neat flipper feet. In her arms she was holding a struggling silver box, and her mischievous grin showed a mouthful of small pearly teeth.

"Oh, thank goodness!" he said. "Where did you find it?"

"Well," she replied, blushing a deeper shade of green, "I saw a big silver box lying about doing nothing. And then I thought the queen might like it for keeping her spare crowns in. So I kind of stole it. Only . . . only then it sort of came alive and told me I'd be in trouble with Poseidon if I didn't bring it back here. So I thought I'd better do what it said. I don't want to be turned into a sea monster! He did that to one of my cousins, and now he's a giant ugly whale thing."

"Just as well," said Demon, a
double surge of anger and relief
shooting through him.

"If I'd lost it, you wouldn't have been the only one Poseidon turned into something horrible." He swam forward and grabbed the box, giving it a little pat of thanks before heading back toward the Hippocamps. The girl followed him.

"What are you doing?" she asked.

"Trying to cure Poseidon's Hippocamps, of course," he said, rather carefully approaching the horse who'd tried to bite him. "Can't you see their scales are all falling off? Now go away. I'm a bit busy, in case you hadn't noticed." The girl didn't move.

"I know the magic Hippocamp trick," she said, watching thoughtfully as the Hippocamp bared its teeth again and laid back its smooth green-bronze ears. "If you're interested." Faster than Zeus's lightning, the horse snaked out its head and clamped its jaws around Demon's arm, its blue eyes rolling.

"Aarrghh!" he yelled, jumping backward and leaving a large chunk of his flesh behind. Immediately, Offy and Yukus slithered off his neck and twined themselves around the wound, sealing and healing it. He turned to look at her. "What magic Hippocamp trick?" he asked, his voice full of suspicion. He wasn't going to trust someone who'd admitted to stealing his magic box *that* easily.

"This," she replied, gliding over to the Hippocamp and seizing it by the nostrils. She brought its head close to her face and blew a stream of bubbles up its nose. At once, its eyelids drooped, and it went all dopey. Demon was impressed in spite of himself. It was as good as his father's magical Pan pipes. The girl turned toward him, a slightly smug look on her face.

"You can examine him properly now. He'll stay calm for a while. I'm Eunice, by the way, daughter of Nereus, and one of the Nereids."

"I'm Demon," he said, holding out a hand. "Official stable boy to the gods on Olympus, and son of Pan. Nice to meet you."

Eunice giggled, holding out her own webbed hand. "We don't do that down here—we wiggle ours instead. But it's nice to meet you, too, Demon. And even nicer that you're not one of my forty-nine stupid sisters. I'm so bored of their fancy jewelry-trying-on parties and silly gossip. I want to do something interesting. I wish I could have a proper job like you—I'd love to look after the Hippocamps. I'd be better at it than those stupid Tritons, anyway!"

"Well, I guess you can help me with this lot, then," Demon said. "But we'd better hurry. I don't want to find out what Poseidon will do if I don't report back to him soon." He turned to the silver box. "I need a cure for these Hippocamps, please." The box began to flash blue as it flapped its fins and moved closer to the still-dopey beast. The see-through skin around the box bulged slightly, and a tube with a suction cup emerged from under the barely open lid, moving over the ragged, peeling scales with a slurping sound before sliding back inside.

"What IS that thing?" asked Eunice, her pale aquamarine eyes widening as she watched.

"Hephaestus made it for me. You know, the smith god? The one who makes all the magic armor for the Olympians? He's really good at inventing stuff." He was about to explain what the box did, when it started to flash and make whirring noises. "Here it goes. We'll have a cure in a minute," he said, crossing his fingers.

"Running preliminary diagnostics," said the box, its tinny tones muffled in the water.

"What's 'preliminary diagnostics'?" Eunice asked.

"Take no notice," said Demon. "It uses fancy terms to make it sound clever, but mostly because it likes to annoy me. 'Diagnostics' just means it's looking for the right medicine." The box spat a blue spark and made what sounded suspiciously like a snort.

"Hipponautikos akropyodermatitis detected in subject," it said. Demon glared at it. "More commonly known as persistent itchy itch."

"Itchy," the Hippocamp whinnied drowsily. Then its eyes snapped open. "ITCHY!" it screamed. "ITCHYitchyITCHYitchyITCHY!" Then it flung itself backward, writhing and wriggling its scales against the pen walls. Immediately, its stablemates joined in, until the whole cave was filled with an echoing chorus of horrible Hippocamp screams and the harsh sound of scales being rubbed off against coral.

CHAPTER 3

A GODLY FIGHT

"STOP IT!" yelled Demon. But it was no good. The
Hippocamps were in a dreadful frenzy of agonizing
itchiness. Neither he nor Eunice could get
anywhere near them to blow soothing bubbles up
their noses—there were too many flailing fish tails
and razor-sharp hooves flying about to even try.
Demon fumbled inside the front of his tunic and
pulled out his dad's magic pipes, hoping against
hope that they'd work underwater. Cramming
them against his lips, he blew hard. A swirl of silver

music curled out, quite visible against the churning turbulence around the terrified sea beasts. The music split into nine parts and shot forward, coiling around each Hippocamp's muzzle like a halter. There was an immediate silence. Every one of the nine panicked creatures sighed deeply, closed its blue eyes, and fell asleep.

"Wow!" said Eunice. "That's way cooler than *my* trick!"

Demon didn't waste a moment.

"Quick, box," he said, "I need a cure right now, before they all wake up again." For once the box didn't argue. The shiny membrane that covered it strained and swelled, and a large copper-colored pot of ointment erupted from its lid with a loud *POP*.

"Apply liberally to all areas," said the box. Then, with a wheezing sound, it closed and shut down. Demon grabbed the pot and wrenched at the lid. It wouldn't budge.

"Come on," he said. "Come ON! Open, you Zeus-blasted thing!"

"Here," said Eunice, swimming forward to help him. "I'll hold, you twist." Demon strained and grunted, and at last, with an earsplitting *CLUNK*, the top came off. As soon as the pot was open, they dug their hands into the gloopy yellow gunk inside and started to smear it over the Hippocamps' scales.

"I really hope this works," said Demon, "because I never want to hear those Hippocamps screaming again. It was AWFUL."

"I know," Eunice agreed, wiping the last of the ointment off her fingers. Just then, the first of the Hippocamps gave a sleepy whinny. Demon crossed his fingers and toes. Could the ointment have

worked so soon? Maybe the Hippocamps would be hungry when they woke up. He looked around him, noticing several bales of silver seaweed piled up in one corner.

"Is that what they eat?" he asked, pointing. Eunice nodded. "Well, at least it's not leftover ambrosia cake," he said. "That would get disgustingly soggy down here." As they swam around, filling each manger, Eunice shot a barrage of questions at him about the Stables of the Gods and Olympus. How many beasts did he have to look after? (A lot.) Why didn't he like ambrosia cake? (Because it was boring eating it day after day, and it didn't taste that nice!) What was the most difficult thing he'd ever had to cure? (Doris the Hydra's cut-off heads.) He hadn't talked so much in ages, and he found he liked being with someone his own age a lot.

"Eunice . . . ," he started. But then all the

Hippocamps woke up at once, plunged their noses into the full mangers, and started munching.

"Look!" she squealed. "They're getting better!" Demon looked. Their scales were gleaming and healthy once more, with tiny new goldy-bronze ones starting to fill in the now-healed pink patches.

"Oh! Thank Zeus's left armpit," he said. Demon glanced down. "Oh, all right. Thank you, too, box." The box glowed a pleased kind of blue and flapped its fins. "Now come on, we'd better go and find one of those Tritons to take us to Poseidon."

Eunice rolled her eyes. "Stupid Tritons. I bet the Hippocamps got sick because those idiots weren't looking after them properly. It wouldn't have happened if I'd been in charge. Don't worry—I'll take you to the throne room. I'd better join my stupid sisters again, anyway, or I'll be in trouble, and that's where they'll be." Chattering on, she led the way upward through the hole in the cave ceiling. Demon followed, trying to copy the graceful, easy way she swam without much success. As he floundered at her heels, he sort of wished Poseidon had given him flippers as well as underwater breathing.

He was concentrating so hard on his swimming that he didn't notice when Eunice stopped dead in front of him.

"OOF!" she gasped as he rammed right into her back, knocking her head over heels through an arched doorway and into a gleaming pool of air and light. Demon suddenly noticed that the water had gotten very hot around him just as Eunice seized him by the hand and dragged him behind a pillar.

"Shh!" she hissed fiercely. "Look!" Demon took a choking breath of damp air and looked about him with wide, awed eyes. He saw a glittering cavern with an endlessly high deep-blue arched ceiling that was decorated with sparkling diamonds to imitate the night sky above the ocean. The smooth walls glowed the exact shade of the inside of a pearly oyster shell. There was a small crowd of sea people and dolphins pressed up against the walls, all looking terrified. In the very center of the room was a high dais with a throne placed on it that seemed to be carved out of one giant sapphire. In front of the throne stood two gods, nose to nose and clearly very angry.

"Say that again!" roared Poseidon, his beard bristling as the water roiled and bubbled around his feet.

"My celestial horses can beat your slow old Hippocamps any day of the week," yelled a purple-robed god who Demon knew must be Helios because of the golden crown of sun rays on his head. Beams of heat shot out from his eyes, turning the light in the cavern orangey-yellow and the water even hotter.

"Gentlegods, gentlegods, there's only one way to settle this," said a voice, apparently coming from nowhere, a voice Demon knew very well. The god Hermes took off his invisibility hat and strolled out of thin air toward the furious gods of sea and sun. "You two must challenge each other to a race. I suggest once around the earth, one of you taking the sea route and the other going by sky. Invite all the gods and goddesses to watch—and the victor gives a feast." The water calmed and became cooler.

"Very well," said Poseidon, stalking back to his throne and sitting down. "Consider the challenge given, Sun Boy."

"Done," said Helios. "I'll meet you seven days from now, Father of Fishiness. Prepare to lose that golden trident of yours!" With that, he let out a blast of blinding light and disappeared.

"Wretched jumped-up Titan," muttered Poseidon,

his eyebrows twitching into a fierce frown. "Always trying to pick a fight." The water in the throne room darkened and began to churn. Several sea nymphs and mermaids squeaked and fled.

"Come on, dear uncle," said Hermes soothingly. "I've seen those Hippocamps of yours. They're fast, and if you rest them well, they should beat Helios easily. Don't forget, those celestial horses of his will be pulling the sun behind them—they won't exactly be fresh."

"Hmm," said Poseidon. "Well, my Hippocamps aren't exactly in top form, either. At least they *weren't*. Maybe Zeus's stable boy has managed to cure them. Where is the wretched brat, anyway? He should have reported in by now." Eunice gave Demon a little shove.

"Go on," she whispered. "Tell him the good news. It might put him in a better temper." Demon swam clumsily forward.

"Er, I'm here, Your Opulent Oceanosity," he said as Hermes winked at him encouragingly. "The Hippocamps are doing well. Their scales are growing back nicely, and they're eating like . . . well . . . horses."

Poseidon scowled at him. "They'd better be fine," he growled, "or I'll have you on your knees scrubbing salt off of seaweed for the next hundred years. Consider yourself assigned to the Stables of the Ocean till further notice. I want my Hippocamps in tip-top condition for the race. You're looking after them full-time till then."

Demon's heart gave a horrible blip and sank right down to his toes. What sort of state would his own Stables be in after a whole week? He'd sworn to the griffin that he'd be back in a couple of days—he didn't trust it and the Nemean Lion to cope for any longer than that, anyway. What WAS he going to do? Giving Hermes a look of complete desperation, he bowed to Poseidon and stammered out the only thing he thought might stop the god from turning him into a coral reef.

"Y-yes, Y-your M-mighty G-godnificence, I'll get down there and see to it at once."

CHAPTER 4

HERMES TO THE RESCUE

"Please, Hermes, please," Demon begged the messenger god silently as he swam slowly back toward where he'd left Eunice. *"I really, really need to talk to you."* But Hermes stayed firmly in the middle of the throne room, chatting away with Poseidon in his usual lighthearted manner. The water was calm and cool again, and he could hear chattering voices ahead of him and squeals of girlish laughter.

"Ooh! Here he is!"

"Isn't he cute?"

"Why don't you introduce us to your *boyfriend*, Eunice?"

Suddenly he was surrounded by a whole gaggle of Nereid girls, each dressed in a different-colored floaty robe. It was like being in the middle of a whole garden of sea flowers. Demon felt himself blushing as Eunice took him firmly by the arm.

"Girls, this is Demon. Demon, these are my sisters, Maira, Neso, Erato, Halia . . ." She stopped. "Oh, never mind. You'll never remember all forty-nine of them, and they're too silly to bother with, anyway." She pulled him out of the circle of admiring glances and giggles, and turned to face them. "Now go away. I've got to show Demon the way back to the stables." Pouting, the pack of girls swam away.

One of them turned back, shaking her finger at Eunice. "Just wait till I tell Amphitrite about you,

Eunice. She'll be cross if you're not there to brush her hair at bedtime. You're meant to be nymph-in-waiting to the queen, not helping some stupid stable boy."

"I don't care, Thetis," said Eunice defiantly. "You know I like being with sea beasts more than brushing royal hair. And he's not stupid. Come on, Demon, let's go." By this time, Demon's face was redder than a ripe cherry. Why did girls always have to be so giggly and weird? Why couldn't they just act normal? He wrenched his arm out of Eunice's grip.

"I'll be fine," he said, horribly embarrassed. "You don't need to come. I can manage to find my own way." Eunice's face fell.

"Oh. All right, then. I just thought . . ." She looked so downcast that Demon immediately felt guilty.

"I didn't mean . . ."

"I only . . . ," they said together.

"You go first," said Eunice, still looking upset.

Demon could see he needed to explain.

"I didn't mean to hurt your feelings," he said. "It's just . . . your sisters . . . Queen Amphitrite . . . I don't want to get you in trouble . . ." He was suddenly not sure what to say.

"Really? Is that all? Oh, never mind them. I told you they were silly, remember? And Queen Amphitrite will let me off, if I explain." Her face turned a deeper green, and Demon realized she was blushing, too. "I-I-I thought it might be because you didn't like me. My sisters always say I'm much too bossy for my own good, but I was only trying to help. I'd really like to be friends with you, if you'll let me." Demon breathed a sigh of relief. "Friends" was just fine by him, and he could definitely use all the help he could get.

"Friends," he agreed, holding out his hand and waggling it at her. "Is this how you do it?"

Eunice laughed. "Pretty much," she said,

flapping her webbed one in return.

The Hippocamps had eaten all their silver seaweed by the time their new friends got down to the Stables of the Ocean. Just then, Demon heard a loud whistle, and Hermes dropped through the hole in the ceiling.

"Fancy seeing you here, stable boy," said the god, his usual mischievous grin spread all over his face. "Did a little fishy whisper that you might be needing me? Are you in trouble AGAIN?"

"Yes," said Demon, too relieved to see him to bother with politeness. "Or I *will* be if I leave the Stables of the Gods with Griffin and Lion in charge for too much longer—and Poseidon wants me to stay here for a whole week. You know what happened the last time."

"I do, indeed. And we can't have the whole of Olympus smelling of poo again, or the goddesses will be after you." Hermes tapped one long fingernail against his very white teeth, clearly thinking. "Tell you what. I have a young man called Autolykos who's in a bit of trouble at the moment over some cattle he stole. He's not bad with beasts, and he owes me a favor or two. I expect he'd look after the Stables for a week. He's a cunning little fellow."

Demon tried to picture a clever thief looking after the giant scorpion, and failed miserably. But what other choice did he have? "Thank you, Hermes," he said gratefully. Then he had an awful thought. What if this Autolykos got badly bitten or even stung by the giant scorpion? He'd need protection. Demon put a hand to his neck and unfastened his magical snake necklace. "Maybe I'd better lend him Offy and Yukus. Otherwise he might get killed. Some of my beasts aren't very friendly, you know. And what about Hephaestus's box?"

"No, no," said Hermes. "You keep all that. I'll make sure he's safe, don't worry. You just get on with looking after these fine beasties. I've got places to be, people to see. Bye for now!" With a wave of his hand, the god put on his invisibility hat and vanished.

"Was that really Hermes?" Eunice whispered. "Only . . . only he doesn't seem like a g—I mean . . ." Her voice stuttered to a halt, but Demon knew exactly what she'd been trying to say.

"Doesn't seem like a god?" he asked. She nodded. "Well, no, he doesn't. At least not like some of the other ones I've met. I'm always scared they're going to turn me into little piles of ash—apart from Heffy and Hestia—but Hermes is really ni—"

Before he could finish his sentence, Eunice, cowering with fear, had darted into a cleft in the rock. A second later he saw why. With a rush of dark water, Poseidon swam into the cave. Demon fell to his knees beside the silver box.

"H-h-hello, Your Serene Saltiness," he said. Poseidon gestured impatiently.

"Get up, get up. All this wretched bowing and scraping drives me mad. Now, let me see how my lovely Hippocamps are doing." Crooning in a most un-king-like way, he went from stall to stall, patting noses and stroking spiky manes. "Well, well. They seem quite recovered." He clapped Demon on the shoulder, sending him shooting backward through the water. "Good job, stable boy. You deserve a reward. Now, let's harness them up and put them through their paces. I'll show you why I'm going to win this race."

Poseidon showed Demon where his racing chariot was, and how to harness the nine Hippocamps to it. Meanwhile, Eunice remained huddled in her rocky hideaway, putting a green finger to her lips. Demon tried not to look at her, not wanting to give her away, as he and the sea god fastened buckles and threaded straps together. Poseidon's help was a big surprise. Hades had made Demon do all the hard work of harnessing the earth dragons, but the king of the sea seemed to like doing it himself. Finally, the chariot was ready.

"In you get," said the sea god, pointing to the seat beside him. Demon climbed in rather nervously. The last chariot he'd been in was Hera's, and that hadn't been a good experience at all. This one was a bit different. It was made in the shape of a long streamlined silver shell, and had two low bucket seats lined with cushions of soft, spongy red sea moss. Poseidon was strapping himself into one with two thick strands of green ribbon kelp, which passed around his shoulders and clipped with two large silver crabs to a third that went between his legs. "Buckle up, stable boy," he barked. "And prepare for the ride of your life."

Scrambling into the second seat beside the king, Demon had just managed to figure out how the kelp harness fitted together when Poseidon swung his trident like a whip, and a jet of blue fire snaked out and cracked over the Hippocamps' heads. With a joyful whinny, they were off. Demon just caught a glimpse of Eunice's scared eyes flashing past before he was jolted back in his seat. He clung to his kelp straps with both hands. The Hippocamps rushed through the golden doors and past the Triton guards, and then Poseidon cracked his trident again.

"Yee-haw, giddyup," he yelled happily, his hair streaming out behind him like weeds. The Hippocamps went even faster, till all Demon could see of the underwater world rushing past him was a series of blurred streaks. Up and up and up they went. Then, with a gasp, Demon was breathing air

again. They were skimming across the top of a calm deep-blue ocean, and the Hippocamps' long, spiky manes flew like golden foam in the breeze.

CHAPTER 5

THE HORSES OF THE SUN

Demon never did manage to catch his breath properly on that wild, amazing ride. Poseidon urged his steeds to go faster and faster. By the time they sank beneath the waves again, Demon's hands were so cramped and uncomfortable from hanging on to his straps that he thought they might never unclench. The sea god looked at him sideways as he slowed the Hippocamps down and guided them gently back into the Stables of the Ocean.

"So, stable boy. How was that for you?"

Demon grinned at the god before he could stop himself. It HAD been very exciting, as well as totally terrifying! "Er, stupendous, Your Serene Saltiness. I think you're going to win. They're really quick, aren't they?"

"Quicker than anything in sea, sky, or earth, and don't you forget it. Now unharness them, and then give them a good rubdown with a sea sponge. Afterward, polish up their scales with some sea-slug slime. They'll need as much seaweed as they can eat. Later we'll take them over to my other palace at Macris. That's where the race is going to start. Got it?" Demon nodded as Poseidon shot up through the hole in the ceiling.

"Yes, Your Mighty Marineness," he said to the god's disappearing toes. Once he was sure he was alone, he peered around him. "Eunice!" he hissed. "Eunice, where are you? You can come out now." But there was no reply. Eunice was gone, and he had no idea where to find her—or any of the items Poseidon had mentioned. There wasn't a sea sponge to be seen anywhere, let alone any sea-slug slime. He led each Hippocamp back to its pen and hung the harnesses up. Pushing the racing chariot back to the small cave it had come from, he wondered what he was going to do. Then he looked at the Hippocamp who'd bitten him, and had an idea.

"Could you tell me where the stable supplies are, please?" he asked politely. But the Hippocamp just rolled its blue eyes at him menacingly and let out a loud whinny.

"Sponge," it neighed. "Slime. Seaweed." Then the whole lot of them started.

"SPONGE. SLIME. SEAWEED," they chorused. They might be fast, Demon thought, but they hadn't so much as a brain cell among them.

"All right, all right! I'll find them myself," he shouted above the noise. But search as he might, he couldn't find anything but the seaweed. With a tired sigh, he tipped it into the mangers to shut the Hippocamps up. He then sat down on a coral ledge next to the silver box.

"Don't suppose you've seen any of that stuff Poseidon mentioned, have you, box?" The box didn't answer, but a beam of blue shot out from its lid, lighting up the murky water in the darkest corner of the stables. Demon saw what looked like a cupboard door in the rocky wall. It had a tiny knob in the shape of a starfish. Wrenching it open, he discovered everything he needed inside.

Armed with sponges, he rubbed down each Hippocamp in turn, using Eunice's clever trick of blowing up the nostrils of any of them who looked like they might nip him. Then he turned to the big pot of sea-slug slime. It was thick and green and gloopy, and if he wasn't careful putting it on the sponge, great globs of it floated off and stuck to his tunic. He was just glad he couldn't smell it, because it looked absolutely revolting. The Hippocamps' scales were fully grown back now, and by the time he'd finished with them, they looked shiny and beautiful, and he was utterly exhausted. It had been a very long day, and he'd had nothing to eat. Curling up on some seaweed in a corner, and trying not to think about his starving stomach, Demon fell fast asleep.

He was woken by a gentle nudge on the shoulder.

"Go 'way, Griffin," he groaned, still half asleep and forgetting where he was. There was another, slightly less gentle nudge to his ribs. Demon's eyes snapped open. There in front of him was a creature with kind eyes and a mouth half open in a friendly grin. It had six starry points of light all along its body, making the whole cavern shine with a warm glow, and it was the most beautiful thing Demon had ever seen.

"Up you get, son of Pan," it said. "Queen Amphitrite wants to see you. Hop on and I'll take you to her." It gestured with a fin to its back. Demon rubbed his sleepy eyes and yawned, wondering what the queen wanted with him, and what this creature was.

"All right," he said. "But I'd better feed this lot first. I don't want Poseidon getting angry with me."

"Wise decision," said the creature. "But hurry up. You don't want to keep the queen waiting, either!" Demon hurried to fill the mangers yet again, then clambered up onto the long, smooth back, hanging on to the big curved fin.

"Er, who are you, if you don't mind me asking?" he said as they swam upward, the powerful body twisting and turning under him, making the lights within it flash and flicker like jewels.

"I'm Delphinus," it said. "Messenger dolphin to the queen. Now hang on and keep your head down. I'm taking us up by the shortcut." Demon ducked low as the dolphin raced this way and that. It moved through narrow tunnels and passageways, eventually shooting out into a brightly lit room. Shafts of sunlight poured in through long, high windows and reflected off a pool of still water, turning it golden. Demon gasped and spluttered as he breathed a sudden rush of real air again. It felt cold and clean and fresh in his lungs.

In the middle of the pool was a large island covered in soft green moss. Demon's heart sank into his sandals as he saw a crowd of brightly colored robes and recognized Eunice's giggling sisters. Reclining on a low couch among them was Queen Amphitrite, with Eunice behind her, brushing out one side of the queen's long dark-blue hair, while her sister Nereid braided tiny jeweled sea anemones into the other.

"Ouch!" cried the queen crossly. "Why do you always have to pull my hair so, Eunice?"

"Here he is, Your Majesty," said Delphinus, giving a wriggle so that Demon tipped off its back and splashed into the golden pool. Amphitrite pointed to a low stool beside her with one webbed finger.

"Swim over and sit there," she said, her voice now low and husky, like tiny pebbles washing against the shore. As Demon clambered out of the water and tried to wring the water out of his tunic, his tummy rumbled loudly. "Are you hungry, son of Pan?"

Demon nodded eagerly. He was hungrier than a starving starfish. "Yes, Your Majesty," he said, trying not to drool too obviously. Amphitrite smiled at him as Delphinus swam off again.

"Halia, fetch our guest something to eat and drink." One of the Nereids went over to a small table, then brought Demon a cup of green juice and a platter piled high with delicious-looking morsels.

"Here you are, Demon," she said, fluttering her long green eyelashes at him in a rather worrying way. Demon was too hungry to care, though. He concentrated on not stuffing everything into his mouth at once instead. He wasn't too sure how goddesses felt about table manners. If Amphitrite was anything like his mom, it was probably best not to gobble like a wild beast.

"I want to know all the gossip from Olympus," said Amphitrite, when he'd cleaned his plate for the third time. "Who's annoyed Hera lately? Is it true about Eos's poor husband? Did Apollo really give that stupid Midas an ass's ears?"

Demon's heart sank into his sloshy sandals. "I . . .

I don't really hear much gossip in the Stables, Your Briny Bountifulness," he said. "Well, only what Althea, Melanie, and Melia say about . . . w-w-well . . ." He stuttered into silence, but Amphitrite just waved a pale-blue webbed hand at him. Her jeweled fingernails flashed in the reflected sunlight.

"Tell me all!" she purred.

"Yes, do," sighed Eunice's sisters, sinking down at the sea queen's feet, like a shower of colorful petals, and gazing up at him expectantly. Blushing, he looked desperately at Eunice for help. She just grinned at him, shrugged, and kept on brushing her royal mistress's hair.

A long and very uncomfortable time later, Amphitrite had wrung out every morsel of information Demon had about the doings of the gods and goddesses on Olympus. She yawned and stretched like a satisfied cat. A loud hooting sounded somewhere outside, making

Demon jump nervously. He was about to ask what it was when he heard a pair of familiar-sounding voices shouting.

"Make way for the Father of Oceans, make way for the King of the Seas," bellowed the Tritons, their monotonous tones ringing around the chamber as they flung open the double doors. Amphitrite rose from her couch, glossy blue hair tumbling down her back like a shiny waterfall. She curtsied and held out a hand to Poseidon.

"Welcome, my king," she said, smiling at her husband.

"Nearly ready to go, my dear?" he asked, striding across the top of the pool toward her, his golden trident strapped across his back. Then his eyes fell on Demon, kneeling at the queen's feet. He frowned, and the room grew darker. Small wavelets began to run around the pool, slapping against the moss. "What's that stable boy doing in your chambers?" he boomed, staring at Demon suspiciously. "He's meant to be looking after my Hippocamps, not lounging about up here!"

"Don't be cross, my cockleshell," said Amphitrite, putting a hand on his arm. "I asked him up here. You know how I get about having the very latest news from Olympus."

"Very well," said Poseidon. "But I want him back now. There's a lot of packing up for him to do before we leave for Macris." He frowned again, but less ferociously. "Off you go, now, boy. I'll send one of the Tritons with you to help." Demon felt a sharp elbow prod his side, and turned to see Eunice glaring at him pointedly. He knew exactly what she wanted him to say before she even mouthed "I want to come" at him.

"Er, Your M-majesties," he said bravely, taking a deep breath and blurting it all out in a rush. "W-would it be all right if I had my friend Eunice as my helper? She's . . . she's very good with the

Hippocamps." Poseidon let out a sudden lightning crack of laughter.

"Good with the Hippocamps, is she, stable boy?" He peered down at Eunice, who was half hiding behind Demon. "Ah! Young Eunice! Aren't you the one my Tritons complain is always hanging about the stables?" Eunice nodded, looking scared. "Well, never mind that . . . You can have her, if my queen agrees . . ." He raised one bushy eyebrow at Amphitrite.

"Oh, very well," she said. "She's already tugged my hair around enough for today. But if there's even a trace of Hippocamp slime anywhere near my best hairbrush tonight, I shall turn you both into a pair of purple clown fish. Now, be off with you."

"Yes, Your Majesty," said Eunice. "I mean, no, Your Majesty. Er . . . I mean, I promise there won't be . . ." Then she curtsied hurriedly, turned, and fled. Demon was close behind her.

CHAPTER 6

THE PALACE OF MACRIS

There was a frantic bustle of activity as Eunice and Demon darted around and dodged gigantic octopus servants holding boxes and baskets. A flurry of sea people rushed this way and that, shouting orders and generally getting in one another's way.

When they reached the stables, the Hippocamps were in a high state of excitement. They neighed loudly and reared as Demon and Eunice ran about packing harnesses, grooming equipment, and bales of silvery seaweed. They used kelp ropes to tie it all onto several long, low sleds that had been left out for them. It took hours and hours. Just as Demon was tying down his silver box (which was shouting loudly that it could perfectly well swim by itself) onto the last sled, several mermen swam in. They led strange long-nosed fish beasts that grinned at them with mouths full of sharp white teeth. Their red backs were covered in arrow-like spines, and huge undulating tails swished the water around their pale, gleaming bellies.

"Ready?" asked one of the mermen in a deep, gruff voice. Demon nodded, backing warily away as the mermen wrangled kelp harnesses around the huge front fins.

"What are *those*?" he whispered.

"Oh, just some of the smaller whale monsters," Eunice said. "They're very friendly, really—as long as you don't feed them oysters. That makes them a bit crazy. My sister Keto is supposed to be in charge of them, but she's so lazy, she lets the mermen do most of the work." She looked over at him as the last sleds floated out of the stables, muffled protests from the silver box still drifting back toward them. "Thanks for letting me come with you. I just wish Poseidon would let me—" She broke off suddenly as Poseidon himself appeared in a swirl of sea foam, and by the time Demon had finished harnessing the Hippocamps to the chariot, Eunice had disappeared again. Maybe he should say something to the sea god about her looking after the Hippocamps. But he had no more time to think about it as the Hippocamps drew them swiftly over the waves to the sea god's earthly home.

Poseidon's above-water palace was a pleasant surprise. Once Poseidon had given him his instructions on how he wanted the Hippocamps fed and exercised for the next few days, Demon started to settle them down in their new homes.

The stables were in a light, airy cave, with spacious stalls where the Hippocamps could splash about to their hearts' content, and with places to store everything else. There was even a tiny alcove above, with a small sleeping pallet and a blanket woven of soft, dry sea grass. Later on, Demon finally set out to explore. It felt good to wiggle his bare toes in the soft, springy grass and feel the herb-scented breeze on his face. Being underwater was all very well for a while, but he definitely missed the smell of fresh air.

Unfortunately, just as he was walking back to see if the sleds of supplies had arrived, he had a nasty surprise. As the sun was setting in a blaze of red and pink clouds, a bright light began to shine on the path in front of him. Demon stopped and stared as the bright light took on the shape of a door, and a tall, dark-haired god with a crown of sun rays stepped out of it. It was Helios, Poseidon's deadly race rival. Demon stared, his mouth hanging open. How in Zeus's name had he done that? Surely even gods couldn't just make doors in the air wherever they wanted?

"Why, if it isn't young Pandemonius," Helios said, baring his white teeth in a friendly grin that somehow looked menacing. "Like my little trick, do you?"

Demon nodded. Well, it *was* pretty amazing.

The god lowered his head. "Not many people know my secret," he whispered. "But I'm sure you'll keep it to yourself. You see, I can make a door anywhere the sun's rays can touch. Useful, eh?"

Demon nodded again as Helios took his elbow in a firm grip so he couldn't escape.

"Now, you're just the boy I wanted. We have important things to discuss." Demon's stomach tried to leap sideways in fright. In his experience, discussing important things with a god almost

always led to the kind of trouble that left him worrying about being frazzled to a frizzle.

"The thing is," said the god, "I have a small problem. Here you are, looking after old Father Fishface's Hippocamps, but, as I understand it, you're the official stable boy to the gods, aren't you? Gods, meaning more than one god . . ."

"W-w-well, y-yes, Y-y-your Sh-sh-shining S-s-serenity." Demon gulped. "I-I s-suppose I am."

Helios smiled again. It was not a nice smile at all. Demon's knees began to tremble. "Oh, good," the god said. "I so hoped you'd say that. You won't mind popping down to the Stables of the Sun for an hour or so, then, and mending one of my celestial horses? Poor Abraxas has gone dreadfully lame, you see. Stepped on a sharp bit of star, or something. I'm sure that magical silver box of yours can fix him in two shakes of a comet's tail, though. Why don't you run along and fetch it, and then we'll be off? Quick as you can, now. I'll be waiting."

Poor Demon! He had no choice, but as he ran back toward where he'd left the Hippocamps, his mind was racing frantically. What if the box hadn't arrived? What if he couldn't cure Helios's horse without it? Even worse, what if Poseidon found out he was working for the other side?

"I'm doomed," he groaned as he ran into the stables, heart thumping like a maenad's drum. "Doomed."

"Why are you doomed?" asked a familiar high little voice. "What's happened now?"

"Oh, Eunice," he said miserably, slumping down onto one of the sleds, which, he was thankful to see, had now arrived. "I don't know what to do." Eunice came to perch beside him as he explained.

"Well," she said, tapping one small pearly tooth with a sharp fingernail, "I don't see what harm it can do if you just go for an hour or two. Cure Helios's horse and come straight back. Poseidon need never know—he and Queen Amphitrite are busy arranging all the stuff for the big party, anyway. I'll start the unpacking and look after the Hippocamps, don't worry." Just then, there was a muffled squawk from behind them. Demon turned around. There was the silver box, wriggling in its seaweed bonds and flashing an angry red.

"Implementing emergency escape mode," it said as several pairs of sharp scissors squeezed out from under its lid and started snipping away at both the kelp ropes and its waterproof cover.

Demon smiled gratefully at Eunice. "Thanks," he said. "You're a . . . a . . . real starfish. I'll be back as soon as I can." Now that he had the box, he was sure he really could cure Helios's horse—maybe things would be okay after all.

"Hello, box," he said, helping it unravel itself

completely and lifting it into his arms as soon as the scissors had retracted. "Come on, we've got work to do." The silver box snarled a cross metallic snarl as Demon ran, bobbing and bumping over the short, springy grass toward the god of the sun. He sighed. The box was clearly in a temper again.

Demon stumbled at the god's heels as they went through Helios's midair door. He felt like he was being bathed in warm spring sunshine. On the other side was a gleaming stable block. Its roof was held up on towering ivory columns. The walls were scattered with glittering flakes of gold and were built of fire-colored marble. The door to each stall was marked with a big bronze flame. Beside the stable, a big flat pasture filled with waving grass and flocks of silvery sheep and goats stretched as far as the eye could see. A truly massive golden chariot was parked by one of the many open barns. Six huge horses had their heads down in the meadow nearby, grazing hungrily, as nymphs bathed the steeds' sweaty sides with water from crystal basins.

"Hey, 'Petia," called Helios. "Bring Abraxas over here, will you?" One of the nymphs set down her basin and led her charge toward Demon and the sun god. Demon could see the big stallion limping badly.

"Oh, dear," he said. "That must hurt."

"It does," whinnied Abraxas pitifully. "A lot."

"Put him in a stall," Helios commanded. "I just need to have another quick word with young Pandemonius here." Demon looked at him nervously. What did Helios want now? The god gripped him by the elbow again, and bent in close. "How are my friends the Cattle of the Sun doing?" the god asked unexpectedly. "Enjoying the nice bales of hay I send up from my fields, are they? Free of stomach gas? Keeping the goddesses happy at the lack of SMELL?"

"Y-y-yes, Your Sparkling Sunniness. Th-th-they're f-fine," Demon stammered, wondering what in Zeus's underpants the Cattle of the Sun had to do with anything. He soon found out.

"Glad to hear it," said Helios. "Now, here's the thing. I might find I have a bit of a problem getting that hay up to Olympus, say, if I heard that old Fish Father's Hippocamps were in tip-top condition for the race. On the other hand, if I heard that they'd had a recurrence of that nasty scale condition—been slowed down a bit by it, if you get my meaning—then I might find that the hay problem disappeared." His grip tightened, and he swung Demon around to face him, piercing him with a bright golden glare. "You understand me, young stable boy?" The god let him go and strode off around the corner of the stables. The nymphs followed. Demon thought he understood only too well. It didn't matter what he did now—whichever god won, he was either fated to be turned into a Demon-size smoking pile of charcoal by goddesses complaining about the terrible smell of gas coming from the Cattle of the Sun's bellies, or doomed to spend the next hundred years scrubbing salt off of seaweed.

CHAPTER 7

DEMON'S DREADFUL DILEMMA

Demon's feet dragged as he slowly approached the lame Abraxas. 'Petia the nymph had left with her sisters, and he was alone with the enormous stallion. "What am I going to do, box?" he asked quietly. The box whirred and flashed blue.

"Random inquiry matrix not enabled," said the box in its normal tinny tones. "Questions of a medical nature only accepted at the present time."

"Some help you are," Demon growled as he flipped the catch on the stall and went inside.

Bending down, he dumped the box on the golden straw and put his hand on Abraxas's lame leg. It was very hot, and the fetlock had swollen up. "Help me with a cure for this, then," he said crossly. The box clicked and whirred as blue symbols flashed on its lid, and then it shot open with a clang, making the stallion back up nervously, half rearing. Demon just barely managed to roll out of the way as a pair of enormous gold-shod hooves clattered past his face.

"Whoa! Whoa!" he said in his most soothing voice, grabbing at the halter. "Calm down, Abraxas. It's only my silly old box having a look at your sick foot. It didn't mean to scare you."

"Well, it did," whinnied a horsey voice high above Demon's head. "Nasty blue thing. I shall kick it, if it does it again." The box scuttled out of the way like a crab, hurriedly dumping a bowl, a pair of tweezers, a big bunch of green bandages, and a large packet of what looked like pink mud at Demon's feet.

"Analysis implemented. Foreign stellar object detected in equine subject. Initiate interactive solution immediately," it said in a snarky metallic gabble. Then it squeezed out of the stall and shut itself down in a sulk. Luckily, Demon had been with the box long enough to understand its strange language.

"You've got a bit of star stuck in your foot, I think," he said, picking up the huge hoof to inspect it underneath. Sure enough, there was something sparkling caught there. Working quickly, he pulled the dazzling fragment of star out gently with the tweezers. He then put a pink mud poultice on the sore part before winding some of the cooling green bandages around the hot fetlock. A large, soft muzzle snorted fragrant hay-scented air down the neck of his tunic.

"Thank you, Demon," Abraxas snuffled. "That feels much better. I must have stepped on a pointy bit of the Milky Way by mistake. Now I shall be able to race perfectly against Poseidon's Hippocamps."

Demon sighed. He'd forgotten about the race for a second.

As Demon led Abraxas slowly into his pasture, the other horses all crowded around.

"We've heard good things about you from our friends the winged horses!" they neighed. "They say you're the best stable boy they've ever had! Can't you come and live with us for a bit? It's boring having no one but the nymphs to talk to. No one ever comes to visit us here. All we ever get to do is pull the sun across the sky—and that's hard work!"

Demon smiled. "I'd love to," he said, "but the gods keep me very busy, you know, and I've got to get back to Poseidon's stables soon." His face fell

as he thought about his problem. "And now your master has asked me to do something awful to the Hippocamps."

"What? What?" they whinnied.

"If I make the Hippocamps ill again," Demon explained, "well . . . I'll . . . I'll be as bad as that horrible Heracles!"

The huge horses began to swish their tails angrily. "Helios can't make you do that," they neighed. "Making beasts sick is wrong."

"I KNOW!" Demon groaned. "But how do I get out of it?"

The horses went into a huddle, nickering softly to one another. Then Abraxas raised his head. "We'll help you stand up to our master, Demon," he whinnied. "But you'll have to be clever. You'll have to trick a god, and so will we."

"I can be clever," said Demon, crossing his fingers in hope that he could. As Abraxas quietly explained their plan, his whiskery muzzle tickled Demon's ear. Maybe this could work. By the time Helios came striding across the pasture, Demon knew exactly what he had to do. He walked forward to meet the sun god, with the six white horses making a solid, comforting line behind him.

"What's this?" said Helios. "You horses all look very serious for this time of night!" He frowned, bright sparks flashing from his eyebrows. "And so do you, young Pandemonius." Demon took a deep breath. Maybe it would be his last, if Helios didn't buy his story. But somehow he didn't care. He'd do what was right, even if he did end up as a pile of ash.

"Well, it's like this, Your Solar Godnificence," he said in a rush. "Your horses and I don't think I should do what you asked. M-my job is making beasts well, not ill. Poseidon would suspect you immediately. B-b-but I think m-maybe I can help you win in another way." He stepped backward into the line of horses and crossed his fingers tightly.

But Helios was looking at his horses.

"Well, my celestial steeds!" he snarled. "And what will you do if I say no to this son of Pan?"

"Then the sun's chariot will not run across the sky till you agree," neighed all six horses together.

"So! Even YOU betray me!" shouted the sun god angrily.

There was a sudden blast of heat, and Demon smelled burning as the edges of his tunic begin to singe and smolder. He began to talk very fast.

"There's a magic herb," he gabbled, batting at the sparks frantically. "It makes beasts run faster than the North Wind if you paint the juice of it on their hooves. I-I can get it for you."

Helios grabbed him and lifted him up by the front of his tunic, leaving his bare legs kicking and dangling. "What is this herb?" he growled. "I've never heard of such a thing."

"I-i-it's c-called G-gorgos Anemos, and it c-comes from the kingdom of the Old Man of the Sea."

Helios threw him down in the grass. "Very well," he growled. "But mark me well, stable boy. If my horses don't run faster than light itself in that race, I will personally see to it that you are set as a spot in the heart of the sun to burn for all eternity!" With that, Helios opened another door in the air and shoved Demon through to Poseidon's island. The silver box came tumbling after him.

Demon gulped and gasped, scrambling and stumbling back down the narrow, rocky path to the stables. The first part of the plan had worked. Now he just had to persuade Eunice to help him with the second, but it would have to wait till the morning. He was too tired to do anything but lie down on his pallet and go to sleep.

A strong smell of seaweed met him as he woke up the next morning. Yawning, he rolled out of bed and jumped down into the stables. The Hippocamps all had their noses buried in their mangers, and Eunice was perched on a rock, playing a little flute crusted with shells.

"Goodness," she gasped, dropping the flute with a crunch. "Whatever happened to your tunic?"

Demon glanced down. There *were* a few big burn holes in it, and some finger-shaped scorch marks. "Helios got a bit angry with me," he said. "I've sort of played a trick on him, and I need you to help me with the next part of it."

Eunice turned pale green. "Me?" she asked nervously. "Why me? What can *I* do?"

"Well," he said, taking a deep breath and hoping.

"Do you by any chance know where the Old Man of the Sea lives?"

Then Eunice did the last thing he expected. She laughed. "Well, of course I do, silly," she said. "He's my dad."

Demon goggled at her. "But . . . but . . . I thought your father was called Nereus!"

"He is. But because he's so ancient and wise, lots of people call him the Old Man of the Sea, too. What do you need him for?"

"Helios's horses told me that a magic herb called Gorgos Anemos grows in his kingdom, and I need it for my trick to work."

Eunice's mouth fell open in shock. "Gorgos Anemos?" Eunice shrieked. "B-but that's our swiftweed flower. No one's supposed to know about that but my family. NO ONE! How did those wretched celestial horses find out about it, by Hades's toenails?" She dived off the rock and swam over to him. "I think you'd better tell me all about this trick you've come up with at ONCE," she said. So Demon explained.

"The horses want it to be a fair race with no cheating," he said. "So although I'm going to paint their hooves with the magic liquid and they'll do what Helios wants and gallop faster than ever before, I'm also going to put it on the Hippocamps' hooves and flippers—only Helios won't know that. So I won't have to make the Hippocamps ill again, and whichever god wins will truly have the honestly fastest team."

"It's still very dangerous," said Eunice. "What if Helios finds out about the family secret? Even worse, if he loses, he's bound to be furious, anyway, and turn you into a sunspot."

Demon thought it was best not to mention at this point that he'd already told Helios about the magic herb—well, how was *he* to have known it was a secret?

"The thing is," he said instead, "Zeus will be at the race, and everyone knows he hates cheating. If Helios loses and comes after me, the horses have promised to threaten him with Zeus's wrath. I-I just have to take the risk. It's only a stupid race, and I won't hurt a beast deliberately, not for any god!"

Eunice sighed. "All right, then. Let's hitch up the Hippocamps and find my dad," she said. "Though if he ever finds out that I'm using the swiftweed for anyone other than family, I'll probably be shut in a cave for a million years and have to marry the giant squid."

CHAPTER 8

THE OLD MAN OF THE SEA

Demon and Eunice harnessed all nine Hippocamps
to the chariot. It was the perfect excuse to exercise
them, just as Poseidon had instructed.

They squashed in, with Demon at the reins,
then shot out of the stables and into the open
air, splishing and sploshing over the crests of the
waves. It was very strange being in the driver's seat,
but Demon soon got used to it, though he didn't
dare go as fast as Poseidon.

"Which way?" he yelled, spitting out a mouthful

of seawater.

"Straight on!" Eunice yelled over his shoulder, her dark-green hair flying in the breeze. Soon Demon began to enjoy himself, and as he got more confident, they went faster and faster, zipping past islands and racing dolphins and sea-skimming seagulls. Then, just as they reached two huge red spires of rock sticking up out of the ocean, Eunice shouted, "Dive!"

They shot downward, then leveled out and

began cantering along a white, sandy road at the
bottom of the sea. Demon held the mass of reins
tightly and kept the Hippocamps going straight.
Looking out of the corners of his eyes, he saw a tall
green forest of kelp trees, their trunks wavering in
the current, and colorful rippling anemones set in
clumps at their roots. Small sea horses, like living
jewels, flitted through the branches. They came

to perch on Demon's head and shoulders, making tiny shrill squeaks of joy. Then the forest thinned, turning into a series of large meadows of sea grass where herds of strange-looking sea monsters with hairy nostrils, crayfish tails, and rows of neat webbed feet were grazing. Then Demon saw a large cave ahead.

"That's my dad's house," said Eunice.

"What should I say?" he asked.

"Leave it to me," said Eunice. "My dad can be a bit funny sometimes. The only thing you have to remember is never to accept his challenge to a wrestling contest. He always wins—and he always cheats!" Demon would have liked to hear more, but Eunice was already slipping out of the chariot and tying the Hippocamps up to a barnacle-encrusted ring.

"Stay there!" Demon said to them sternly as he scrambled out after her. The Hippocamps looked at him sideways, put their heads down, and started tearing up sea grass.

"Hey, Dad! Where are you? It's me, Eunice! I've brought a friend to visit," she called, swimming into the cave. Demon followed clumsily after her. The cave was dimly lit by angler fish set in niches in the walls. It had a far more homey feel than Poseidon's palace. There were bits of wrecked ships serving as chairs and tables, and some rather rickety shell ornaments—clearly made by Eunice and her sisters—dotted the floor and the driftwood shelves.

"In here," came a booming voice.

"This way," Eunice hissed, beckoning Demon into a smaller cave. Stooped over a pile of black horned objects was the Old Man of the Sea. His long hair was tied back with a string of bladder wrack, and his beard was knotted with shells and small starfish. In his hand he had a large needle threaded with an array of sparkling jewels. Eunice grinned.

"Decorating purses for the mermaids again, Dad?" she asked. Nereus grunted.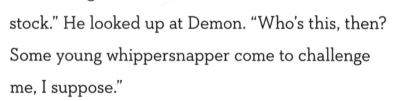

"Careless girls are always losing 'em," he said. "I never have enough in stock." He looked up at Demon. "Who's this, then? Some young whippersnapper come to challenge me, I suppose."

"No! Of course not, Dad. This is Demon, Pan's son. He's looking after Poseidon's Hippocamps for now, but he's really the stable boy to Olympus. He's a great healer, too."

Nereus looked at Demon from under bushy eyebrows. "You sure you don't want to wrestle me, son?"

Demon shook his head, remembering what Eunice had told him. "Not really, thank you very much, Your Ancientness. I'm a bit short for it."

"Well, you're no Heracles, that's for sure. Wretched heroes—I hate 'em. Always wanting something for nothing. Suppose you want something, too, do you?" Demon was about to answer when Eunice trod hard on his toe with one of her flipper feet.

"No, no," she said airily. "Demon just wanted to see where I used to live. We were exercising the Hippocamps and thought we'd drop by for a visit. But now that you mention it, I could do with a bit of swiftweed juice for my dolphin. Poor old Seapetal's fins are getting a bit creaky. We can't keep up with my sisters anymore, so I want to rub some on him before we go for our next ride." She beamed up at her father lovingly. "I know you don't give it out to just anybody, but surely I can have some. I am your favorite daughter, after all!" Nereus stared at her suspiciously.

"Swiftweed juice, eh? Dangerous stuff, that. You be careful with it. Use a seagull-feather brush to put it on like I taught you, and don't use too much, or the poor beast will take off like a rocket." He glared ferociously at Demon. "And don't you go telling anyone about it, either, young Demon. It's meant to be a family secret, that juice is, and Eunice here had no business talking about it in front of you. If that wretched Heracles or any of the other heroes get to hear about it, I'll have them tromping down here in droves, wanting some to make their stupid arrows fly faster, or something."

"Don't worry, I'd never tell anyone. I don't like Heracles, either," said Demon. "He's always bashing up my beasts."

"Well, see that you don't. Or I'll turn you into a clam." The Old Man of the Sea moved across to a large alcove set in the rock and picked up a crystal jug full of bright orange liquid.

"Here," said Eunice, pulling out a large bottle with a carved stone stopper from inside her robe. "You can put it in this." She reached up and gave him a kiss on his hairy cheek. "Thanks, you're the best dad in the world."

"You and your little tricks." He chuckled, handing her the filled bottle. "Now get away with you, child, and give my love to your sisters. Tell them to come visit soon. Amphitrite keeps all of you too busy!"

"I will," said Eunice, pulling Demon out of the cave and toward the tethered Hippocamps. "I promise." She put her finger to her lips as soon as they were around the corner and out of sight. "Don't say anything. The walls have ears," she whispered, nodding toward the angler fish lights.

Eunice slipped out of the chariot as soon as

they drove into the palace stables. "I'd better go and check on Amphitrite. She said I still had to do my duties for her, even if I was helping you. I'll be down again as quick as I can—sorry to leave you with all the work." Fumbling in the pocket of her robe, she thrust the bottle of swiftweed juice at him. "Hide this in a safe place, and DON'T use it till I can show you how." Then she shot off before he could say a single word. Demon shoved the bottle under a bale of silver seaweed as the Hippocamps began to prance and dance with impatience to get to their mangers. He'd deal with it later.

Demon felt a bit lonely once he'd finished seeing to the Hippocamps. They weren't very good company—they only spoke in single words, and he missed the griffin's snarky chat. He got out the bottle of swiftweed juice and looked over at the box, which was still on the high rocky shelf where he'd left it. "Box," he said politely. "Would you mind keeping this safe for me? It's pretty dangerous stuff, apparently, and I need to make sure that nobody but Eunice or me uses it."

The silver box shuddered and let out a couple of blue sparks, but eventually its lid opened with a cross-sounding creak. "Insert object," it said, rather grudgingly. Demon placed the bottle inside, and immediately the lid snapped shut. The box began to hum busily. "Poison protocols in process," it announced, just as a flashing red skull and crossbones appeared on each of its sides. Demon patted it, then yelped as a strange tingly shock passed through his hand.

"Ouch!" he yelled.

"Safety procedures present and correct." The box glowed. "Item now password protected."

"Password?" asked Demon angrily, sucking his sore fingers. "What's the password?"

"Mother's name plus father's gift," it whirred.

Demon thought for a moment, puzzled. Then it suddenly came to him. "Er, that would be . . . er . . . Carys and Pan pipes," he said.

"Correct. Do you wish to retrieve item?"

"No, not now. You keep it safe. Thanks, box. You're the best." The box glowed bright blue with pleasure.

CHAPTER 9

THE SWIFTWEED TEST

The stables were spick and span; the Hippocamps were happy, polished, exercised, and fed. Demon wondered what to do next. He wasn't used to having only one set of beasts to look after. Should he try to find Eunice? Should he report to Poseidon? Or should he find the kitchens? Since he was now hungrier than a pack of ravening manticores, and his stomach was in danger of sticking to his spine, he decided that finding the kitchens was pretty urgent.

"I don't suppose you know where the kitchens are," he asked the Hippocamps.

"KITCHENS! FOOD! YUM!" they squealed. Demon rolled his eyes.

"You're hopeless," he sighed. "I guess I'll have to find them myself." But just then, Eunice came into the stables with five of her sisters. They were all riding dolphins, and Eunice had another one on a silver rein.

"Come on, Demon," she called. "I've brought Seawhistle for you to ride. Amphitrite wants us to collect some shells for decorating the banqueting hall. There's a perfect beach on the island next door." Unfortunately, Demon's stomach gave an enormous gurgle right as she stopped talking, and the Nereids all giggled.

"I think he's hungry again," said the one in the pink robe.

"Poor boy," said the one in yellow. "Haven't you

been feeding him, Eunice?" Demon felt his face getting redder than the setting sun as he climbed onto Seawhistle's back.

"I can perfectly well feed myself!" he snapped, wriggling himself into place behind the big back fin. "It's just that I haven't quite found out where the kitchens are yet."

Eunice laughed. "Well, that's easy enough," she said. "Let's go there before we start on the shells."

The palace kitchens were amazing. Pots and pans full of delicious-looking things bounced and boiled on top of jets of scalding water, and piles of strange-looking sea vegetables were being chopped and shaped and stuffed, along with endless baskets of shellfish. There was even a huge cotton candy castle being decorated with edible shells and strands of seaweed. Poseidon's cooks seemed to be preparing enough food to feed a thousand gods and goddesses, and Demon's stomach was soon as full as it could be. Afterward, he found himself collecting shells on a little white sandy beach. The Nereids thought it was funny to pelt him with wet seaweed, but he soon repaid them by stuffing sand down the backs of their robes.

After that, Demon quickly fell into a routine. What with exercising the Hippocamps in the morning, getting them ready for Poseidon's daily inspection, then taking time off in the afternoons to ride Seawhistle and explore with Eunice and the other Nereids, the days before the race quickly passed. Despite what Eunice said about her sisters, they were fun to be with, always laughing and playing jokes as they showed him around the palace, challenged him to swimming races (which he always lost), and generally treated him like a long-lost younger brother. But the night before the race, he started to get a nasty sinking feeling of doom in his stomach.

As he was giving the Hippocamps their last feed, he was surprised to see Eunice ride in on her dolphin, Seapetal, with Seawhistle swimming behind her. By that time he had rumpled his hair into a tangled bird's nest.

"What are you doing here?" he asked, as nasty, wriggly worry things joined the feeling of doom. "Is-is-is something wrong?"

"No, nothing's *wrong*, except that my sisters are all fluffing and faffing and looking at stupid jewels," she said. "Luckily, Amphitrite is too busy choosing which dress to wear tomorrow to notice I'm not there, so I thought I'd escape. Want to take Seawhistle for a night ride? There's a lovely full moon, and the stars are much brighter than Halia's silly old opals." Then she frowned, looking at him. "What's the matter, Demon? Why is your hair all sticky-uppy like that?"

"What if the swiftweed juice doesn't work?" he burst out. "What if it's a bad batch or something? What if Poseidon and Helios find out? What if the effect runs out halfway through the race . . . ?" Eunice rode over and grabbed his shoulder, giving him a little shake.

"You big silly," she said. "Of course it'll work—it lasts for a whole day, usually. And I'll be there to help with the Hippocamps. You'll see—it'll all be fine. But if you're really worried, we can try out a tiny drop on Seapetal and Seawhistle here. They won't tell anyone, will you, boys?" The dolphins opened their mouths and grinned, shaking their heads violently.

"Race you," they whistled to each other. "Last one back's a barnacle's bottom!"

Eunice was very impressed with the box's security measures. "It's better than a whole legion of those stupid Triton guards," she said as the bottle of swiftweed appeared, making the box glow with pleasure again. Taking a tiny seagull-feather brush from her pocket, she dipped just the very tip into the bottle and painted a minuscule amount onto the dolphins' front flippers and tails before putting everything back.

"Now," she said, jumping onto her dolphin's back, "let's race." Demon hardly had time to scramble onto Seawhistle before Eunice and Seapetal shot out of the stables faster than Zeus's lightning bolts. Seawhistle followed, streaking past his friend as Demon clung on for dear life. Right out into the ocean they raced, following the silvery path of the full moon. The stars zipped past in a blur overhead as the dolphins whistled and clicked with glee, overtaking shoals of very surprised-looking fish, and jumping high in the air. By the time they turned back, Demon had no more worries about whether the swiftweed would work or not. It was fantastic stuff! But as they came into view of the palace, they saw an extraordinary sight. A column of rainbow-colored light streamed down from the moonlit heavens and into the palace, lighting up the sky. Demon reined Seawhistle to a halt, Eunice slowing beside him.

"Whatever is THAT?" asked Eunice, shading her eyes.

"Gods!" Seawhistle whistled, dancing among the waves.

"Goddesses!" clicked Seapetal. "Lots of them."

Demon recognized the multicolored light. "It's the Iris Express from Olympus. I'd better start getting the Hippocamps ready. Poseidon will be coming to get the chariot soon." He gulped. "I-I just hope Helios doesn't arrive at the same time."

"Oh no!" gasped Eunice. "I've got to get back to the queen. If the gods and goddesses are arriving already, Amphitrite will definitely notice that I'm not there. She's bound to be fussing that Aphrodite has a better dress for the feast, or something stupid. Come on, Seapetal, quick! I'll see you later, Demon—and DON'T WORRY!" Her voice faded into the distance as Demon headed more slowly to the stables.

Even though Demon knew now that the swiftweed worked, he was still nervous. To keep himself occupied, he polished the sleepy Hippocamps over and over till their bronze scales shone. Even the fiercest one was used to him now, and it nuzzled his pockets for the purple seaberry treats he'd taken to bringing them from the kitchen. Just as he was going to get the harnesses ready, there was a blaze of light in the cave entrance.

"Time to keep your promise, stable boy," Helios said as he appeared through his door in the air, smiling his dangerously white smile. "I do hope you succeeded in getting what you needed from the Old Man of the Sea. It would be such a shame to turn you into a sunspot when it seems you've worked so hard polishing up those stupid sea steeds for his Foolish Fishiness." He smirked. "It won't help them go faster, though, will it?"

"N-no, Your Sunshiny Superbness. It definitely

won't." It wasn't a lie, Demon thought. Shininess *wouldn't* help the Hippocamps go faster. "I-I'll just go g-g-get the magic juice." Taking a deep breath to calm himself, he whispered the password to the box, got the swiftweed juice out, and put it safely inside his robe, together with the seagull-feather paintbrush. "Ready," he said, scrambling up onto the rock, hoping that Poseidon wouldn't come to the stables and find him gone. Helios grabbed his hand and pulled him through the door to the other side. Waiting just outside were the six golden-maned celestial horses, each with a nymph at its head. They were already harnessed to the gigantic Chariot of the Sun, which had a long braided rope snaking out behind it into the distance. Demon could see the top of a shining golden ball just poking over the horizon.

"Hurry up, boy," snapped Helios. "Dawn waits for no god, and she'll be going to the starting line soon." He seemed nervous, but not as nervous as Demon, whose hands were shaking as he brushed each shining golden hoof with a drop of swiftweed juice. Abraxas bent his head and brushed Demon comfortingly with his white muzzle, but he didn't say anything. It was too dangerous with Helios so near. Finally Demon finished and stood up. The horses were now pawing restlessly at the ground, their skins rippling and shuddering.

"All done, Your Celestial Cloudlessness," he said, stuffing the bottle and brush back into his tunic. Helios stepped forward, leaning over him until they were nearly nose to nose. Demon could feel the heat of the sun god's gaze singeing his eyebrows, but he didn't dare move.

"And can you swear to me that they'll run faster than they ever have before, stable boy?" he asked softly, his voice as menacing as the giant scorpion's sting.

"Y-y-yes," Demon stammered. "Faster than the North and South Winds together, I swear. You'll notice the difference in them immediately." He just hoped the Hippocamps would run equally as fast.

"They'd better, or you'll be a crispy sunspot by sundown!" With one last threatening glare, Helios pushed Demon back through the door.

"I wish his own sun would burn him to a crisp," Demon muttered angrily. "I'm fed up with gods pushing me around and bullying me." He went to get the harnesses in a very grumpy mood.

CHAPTER 10

THE RACE OF SEA AND SUN

As Demon finished polishing the very last buckle, Poseidon whirled into the cave, golden trident in hand, his beard bristling and crackling with energy.

"Good, good," he said. "Glad to see you've got everything in tip-top condition early, Pandemonius. We don't want to be outshone by those celestial beasties, do we?"

Demon shook his head. "Definitely not, Your Marine Magnificence," he said.

"You can bring the chariot around to the east side of the island now. Eos is going to start the race just as dawn breaks. We're going to show that stupid Sun Boy show-off who's fastest, aren't we, my lovelies?" said the sea god as he visited each Hippocamp's stall.

"GO FAST! FAST! FAST! FAST!" they trumpeted, beginning to rear and plunge.

"Calm down, calm down! Save your energy for the race!" Poseidon boomed, patting Demon on the shoulder. "I'll see you there, stable boy. Now I've got to go and greet my fellow gods." He frowned. "Not my kind of thing, but Amphitrite insists we do things properly. Says Olympus will look down on us if we don't." With that, he disappeared in a sparkling whoosh of seawater.

Should he put the swiftweed juice on the Hippocamps now? Demon wondered. No. That wouldn't do at all. Helios was bound to think it was suspicious if they galloped up to the starting line too fast. He'd have to sneak it on at the last minute without Helios seeing. His heart began to thunder like a whole herd of centaurs. However was he going to pull this off?

With trembling fingers, he harnessed the excited Hippocamps to the chariot, then got in and headed for the east side of the island. Driving up onto a shallow beach in the gray light before the dawn, he jumped out and stood ready by the Hippocamps' heads. Up on the cliff above was a huge crowd of gods and goddesses seated on a bank of seats covered in silken cushions. Craning his neck, he spotted Zeus's crown of lightning bolts—and was that Hera beside him, waving a fan of peacock feathers and talking to Poseidon and Amphitrite? He scuttled around to the other side of the Hippocamps. He didn't want *her* spotting him! Then he noticed something else. Making her way down the cliff path was a tall goddess dressed in palest pink. Eos, goddess of dawn, was on her way to start the race. He looked around him frantically. Where was Eunice? He couldn't do this without her help, and time was running out!

Luckily, just then, a breathless Eunice swam up on Seapetal. "Have you put it on them?" she hissed at him as she slid off the dolphin's back.

"No," said Demon. "Helios's horses are done, but I haven't had a chance to do the Hippocamps yet. I was waiting for you. Quick! Hold on to them while I pretend to inspect their hooves and tails." Working fast, and keeping a nervous eye out for Helios and his chariot, Demon daubed a drop of swiftweed juice onto each tail, fin, and hoof. Just as he'd finished the last Hippocamp, he saw Poseidon striding toward him across the sand. He shoved the bottle and brush back into his tunic as the Hippocamps beside him started to act even more like high-strung thoroughbreds than usual. Their front hooves were pawing at the sand, and their tails thrashed the water behind, making the chariot toss and sway in the waves. The swiftweed was definitely taking effect! Demon held the chariot steady as Poseidon climbed in.

"Whoa!" he yelled as the Hippocamps plunged and reared with impatience to be off. "Whoa, you eager beasties!" He waved frantically to Eos as a tiny rim of light appeared on the horizon, six white horses silhouetted against its brightness. Helios had arrived! "Ready when you are, Sun Boy," Poseidon shouted, voice booming across the waves as he raised his trident. "I can hardly hold mine back—you don't have a chance with those celestial nags of yours!"

The sun god laughed rudely. "Eat my spray, Fish Father!" he yelled back, cracking his starry whip so that his horses reared in their traces.

On your marks," shouted Eos, raising her arms in the air. "Get set! GO!" Out of her fingers shot beams of pink radiance, which lit up the whole sky.

The Hippocamps hurtled forward in a froth of foam, just as Helios's team streaked away in the distance. Within seconds they were out of sight over the western horizon, roared on by a crowd of gods standing on the hill above the shore and a cheering mass of sea folk bobbing in the waves. The race was on!

"Let's go and find my sisters," said Eunice. "You can't do anything more now, and we might be able to see more from up there." Together, they climbed the little path up the cliff, Eunice stumbling a bit on her flipper feet. Demon grabbed her arm as she nearly tripped on a rock.

"Oops!" she said, wincing. "I'm not really used to walking on this stony stuff. It feels like knives digging into me." Demon hadn't really thought about that.

"Do you want a piggyback ride?" he asked.

"Yes, please!" she said gratefully. So Demon,

wheezing and panting a bit, carried her up the cliff. She was a lot more solid than she looked, and he was quite glad to set her down on the soft grass at the top. Squeezing past a mass of nymphs and fauns who were chattering and shoving each other and standing on tiptoe to see something just in front of them, Eunice and Demon ended up by the crowd of seated gods and goddesses. Zeus was standing on a disk of air in front of them, his hands creating what looked like a picture in the air—a huge revolving blue globe, with white at the top and bottom, and lots of large, green, strangely shaped blobs set in the blue bits. Two fiery dots—one gold, one silver—were moving across it, leaving a trail behind them. The gold dot was slightly in front of the silver one, and the two trails led back to one flashing red beacon. All the gods and goddesses were yelling for their favorites.

"Come on, Poseidon," shouted a deep voice

just above Demon's head. He looked up and saw a familiar figure with a black beard and a dirty face. It was his friend Hephaestus! He reached up and tugged on the smith god's robe.

"Hello, Heffy," he called. Hephaestus looked down, frowning, but when he saw Demon, his soot-stained face broke into a broad grin.

"Well, if it isn't young Pandemonius," he said. "What are you doing down there, you cheeky brat? And who's your friend?"

Demon introduced Eunice, who smiled nervously.

"Ah, one of the Nereids, are you?" said the smith god, nodding his head wisely. Then he turned back to Demon, a stern look on his face. "There's been an awful lot of noise coming from the Stables lately, young man—you should keep those beasts of yours under better control."

"I haven't been there," he said, hastily explaining

about Poseidon and the Hippocamps. "Hermes was supposed to send someone called Autolykos to look after the beasts." He looked worried. "Maybe he hasn't been looking after them properly. Er, there hasn't been a smell of . . . you know . . . has there?"

"What, poo? Not that I've noticed," said Hephaestus. He looked over at Zeus's picture. "Come ON, Poseidon," he roared, shaking his fist in the air.

"Er, excuse me, Your Godnificence," said Eunice timidly. "What is that round thing?"

"That? Why, that's a picture of the whole world, of course, sea child." He pointed to the two moving dots. "There's Poseidon, see? He's the silver dot. And there's Helios. He's the gold dot. Where we are now is the red dot—and that's the start and finish line. Zeus is judging the race, you know—and this way we can all see there's no cheating." He cleared his throat and looked around, lowering his voice slightly. "I've wagered Ares one of my magic suits of armor that Poseidon will win. He's supporting Helios, of course, but I reckon Poseidon has the edge. Helios's horses are ahead now, but they've got that heavy sun to pull, remember, and I think they'll be all out of steam by dusk." Demon said nothing, but he heaved a deep sigh. He was pretty much in trouble, whichever god lost.

The lead changed several times throughout that long day. Finally, the silver and gold trails were almost at the red dot again, and as the sun sank toward the west, the gods and goddesses cheered even louder, shaking the earth with their cries. Demon's heart began to pound in his chest. Helios's gold dot was just in front, but Poseidon's silver one was creeping up on it. Then, with a flash of light, the two teams burst over the eastern horizon. Zeus raised his hand, and a bolt of lightning sizzled and hissed as it hit the waves, laying out a long red finish line in front of the two teams of galloping steeds. Poseidon's trident streamed with blue fire, which whipped out over the Hippocamps' heads, as Helios urged his horses on with a crack of starlight. Slowly, inch by inch, the Hippocamps were catching the celestial horses, and Demon found his fists were clenched so hard that his fingernails dug painfully into his palms.

"Come on, come on, come ON," he muttered as Eunice shrieked and danced beside him. With a last, mighty effort, the Hippocamps drew level with their rivals, and as their noses touched the lightning finish line, two identical spears of red flame shot into the air beside each chariot.

Zeus's voice boomed like thunder as Helios and Poseidon reined their steeds to a halt. "I declare this race a DEAD HEAT!" he roared into a sudden silence. "You have BOTH won!"

Poseidon and Helios began to laugh at the

same time. "Good race, Sun Boy!" said the sea god, reaching over and holding out his hand to his rival deity.

"Good race, Fish Father," said Helios, leaning over and shaking it firmly. "The four Winds themselves couldn't have beaten either of us today. My horses have NEVER run so fast." His eyes sought out Demon in the crowd, and as the sun god gave him a nod, Demon felt a big burden of fear slip from his shoulders. He wouldn't be a sunspot or have to scrub seaweed after all!

CHAPTER 11

THE ORDER OF OCEAN

"Let us care for our gallant beasts," said Poseidon, raising his trident, "and then we will feast and salute each other's victory." Demon knew that was his signal. Heading down the cliff path again, he ran to the Hippocamps' heads. Their sides were heaving, and they looked tired, but Demon could see they were happy.

"HOORAY! HOORAY! HOORAY!" they whinnied as Helios and his horses finally pulled the sun beneath the horizon and dusk fell.

Poseidon clapped Demon on the shoulder. "Well done, stable boy," he said. "We didn't win, but we didn't lose, either. I've never known them to go so quick as they did today. Whatever you've been doing to them, it certainly paid off. Don't suppose I can persuade you to stay here and look after them full-time, can I?"

"Well, Your Mighty Marineness, I'd love to, really," said Demon carefully, "but I don't think Zeus would be very happy about it, and it wouldn't be fair to my beasts up on Olympus."

"Well, I suppose not. But if they get sick again, I'll be calling on you. You can be sure of that. Now take these poor beasties back to their stalls and give them a good feed and a rubdown. Then come back to the feast. You deserve a reward for all your hard work."

"SEAWEED! SPONGE! SLEEP!" neighed the Hippocamps eagerly as they galloped around the island to their stable. Demon took care of them, then made his way up to the banqueting hall, wiping the worst smears off his tunic as he went.

It was as magnificent as the undersea throne room. The towering walls were banded with stripes of lapis lazuli and mother-of-pearl, and under the pale-blue crystal ceiling, sparkling yellow stars whirled and shone, speckling the room with twinkles of moving light. Water lapped around tall columns of white coral, and on a raised dais carved with sea creatures was an enormous shell-decorated silver table where the gods and goddesses were sitting. Smaller silver tables led down in a series of steps from each end of the big table, eventually dipping down into the water so that the sea folk could eat comfortably.

Demon looked around the noisy room buzzing with chatter. Where should he sit? Then he spotted Eunice and her Nereid sisters, who were waving and beckoning from a table just below the dais. "Over here, Demon," they called.

Helios had decided that as he was joint victor, he'd bring half the feast from his kitchens. There was stuff Demon had never eaten before, but it all looked yummy. He wasted no time in filling his plate.

The evening passed in a blur of eating and drinking, and just as Demon was stuffing in one last morsel of sun cake, Poseidon banged on the floor with his trident. The whole banqueting hall shook.

"Brother Zeus," he said loudly. "I have borrowed your stable boy, and much as I should like to keep him, I must return him to Olympus. But first, I would like to reward him. Stand forth, Pandemonius, son of Pan."

Demon nearly choked. "What, me?" he whispered to Eunice. She gave him a little push.

"Yes, you! Go on, don't keep him waiting!"

Demon wriggled under the table and walked

up the steps, sandals sloshing slightly and very aware of his slightly grubby tunic, to kneel in front of Poseidon's seat. He didn't dare look up, with so many gods and goddesses staring at him.

"You have done me great service, son of Pan, and I hereby award you the Order of Ocean, and the freedom of my seas. You may also ask a reward of me." Demon did look up at that, totally amazed.

Poseidon was holding out a large speckled cowrie shell with golden edges, hanging from a heavy golden chain. Demon scrambled off his knees and leaned forward so the sea god could hang it around his neck.

"Now, Pandemonius, what reward can I give you? Jewels, pearls—perhaps some golden treasure?" Demon shook his head, speechless. He didn't need any of those things. Then he caught a glimpse of Eunice, and suddenly he knew exactly what he was going to ask for.

"Well, Your Serene Saltiness, maybe there's one thing. C-could you possibly make my friend Eunice the official Keeper of the Hippocamps? The Tritons don't seem that interested in looking after them, a-and Eunice is really very good with them and the d-dolphins—m-much better than she is at brushing hair." He stopped abruptly, aware that he was babbling a bit.

Poseidon laughed. "Very well," he said. "Come here, young Eunice. I can't say I'm very surprised after all the times my Amphitrite has complained about you running away to hang around my stables!" Eunice came up to the dais, beaming like the midday sun, and stopped by Demon's side.

"From this moment forward, Eunice the Nereid is official Handmaid to the Hippocamps and Damsel of the Dolphins," Poseidon announced, and the room erupted in loud claps and cheers as Demon and Eunice made their way back to their table, where Eunice's sisters were clapping loudest of all.

"Thanks," she whispered to Demon. "A proper job at last! I'm so happy, I could pop like a squashed sea slug!"

"Ugh! Gross!" he whispered back. But he didn't really mean it. He was too happy himself. Tomorrow he'd go back to the Stables on Olympus and sort out whatever mess Autolykos had made of them, but tonight . . . tonight he was going to celebrate his lucky escape from sunspots and seaweed-scrubbing with Eunice and all his new Nereid friends.

GLOSSARY

PRONUNCIATION GUIDE

THE GODS

Aphrodite (AF-ruh-DY-tee): Goddess of love and beauty and all things pink and fluffy.

Apollo (uh-POL-oh): The radiant god of music. More than a little sensitive to criticism.

Ares (AIR-eez): God of war. Loves any excuse to pick a fight.

Eos (EE-oss): The Titan goddess of the dawn. Makes things rosy with a simple touch of her fingers.

Hades (HAY-deez): Zeus's brother and the gloomy, fearsome ruler of the Underworld.

Helios (HEE-lee-us): The bright, shiny, and blinding Titan god of the sun.

Hephaestus (hih-FESS-tuss): God of blacksmithing, metalworking, fire, volcanoes, and most things awesome.

Hera (HEER-a): Zeus's scary wife. Drives a chariot pulled by screechy peacocks.

Hermes (HUR-meez): The clever, fun-loving, jack-of-all-trades messenger god.

Hestia (HESS-tee-ah): Goddess of the hearth and home. Bakes the most heavenly treats.

Pan (PAN): God of shepherds and flocks. Frequently found wandering grassy hillsides, playing his pipes.

Poseidon (puh-SY-dun): God of the sea and controller of natural and supernatural events.

Zeus (ZOOSS): King of the gods. Fond of smiting people with lightning bolts.

OTHER MYTHICAL BEINGS

Amphitrite (am-fih-TRI-tee): Poseidon's wife and queen of the sea. A pretty high-maintenance lady.

Autolykos (ow-TOL-ih-kohs): A trickster who shape-shifts his stolen goods to avoid getting caught.

Delphinus (dell-FY-nuss): A messenger dolphin who helped play matchmaker between Poseidon and Amphitrite.

Heracles (HAIR-a-kleez): The half-god "hero" who just loooves killing magical beasts.

Midas (MY-dus): A king who foolishly wished for everything he touched to turn to gold.

Naiads (NYE-adz): Fresh-water nymphs—keeping Olympus clean hs who love to gossip.

Nereus (NEER-ee-uss): The Old Man of the Sea. Though, with fifty daughters, they ought to call him the Old Dad of the Sea.

Nymphs (NIMFS): Giggly, girly, dancing nature spirits.

Tritons (TRY-tunz): Fish-tailed guards with human torsos. Probably also have fish brains.

PLACES

Macris (mahk-REES): Big island off mainland Greece, shaped like a sea horse. Where Poseidon has his above-water palace.

BEASTS

Abraxas (uh-BRAK-suss): One of Helios's immortal horses, destined to pull the sun across the sky forever.

Centaur (SEN-tor): Half man, half horse, and lucky enough to get the best parts of both.

Cerberus (SUR-ber-uss): Three-headed guard dog whose only weaknesses are sunshine and happiness.

Griffin (GRIH-fin): Couldn't decide if it was better to be a lion or an eagle, so decided to be both.

Hippocamp (HIP-oh-camp): Beast with a horse's head and a fishy tail. Like a sea horse, but bigger, scalier, and dumber.

Hydra (HY-druh): Nine-headed water serpent. Hera somehow finds this lovable.

Manticore (MAN-tik-or): A spiky, hairy, hungry, lion-like, man-eating monster with a tail like a scorpion or snake.

Nemean Lion (NEE-mee-un): A giant, indestructible lion. Swords and arrows bounce off his fur.

ABOUT THE AUTHOR

Lucy Coats studied English and ancient history at Edinburgh University, then worked in children's publishing, and now writes full-time. She is a gifted children's poet and writes for all ages from two to teenage. She is widely respected for her lively retellings of myths. Her twelve-book series Greek Beasts and Heroes was published by Orion in the UK. Beasts of Olympus is her first US chapter-book series. Lucy's website is www.lucycoats.com. You can also follow her on Twitter @lucycoats.

ABOUT THE ILLUSTRATOR

As a kid, **Brett Bean** made stuff up to get out of trouble. As an adult, Brett makes stuff up to make people happy. Brett creates art for film, TV, games, books, and toys. He works on his tan and artwork in California with his wife, Julie Anne, and son, Finnegan Hobbes. He hopes to leave the world a little bit better for having him. You can find more about him and his artwork at www.2dbean.com.